PETER POWERS

and the
League of
Lying Lizards!

PETER POWERS™

and the League of Lying Lizards!

By Kent Clark
& Brandon T. Snider
Art by Dave Bardin

Little, Brown and Company

New York Boston

Copyright © 2017 by Hachette Book Group, Inc.
PETER POWERS is a trademark of Hachette Book Group.
Cover and interior art by Dave Bardin
Cover design by Christina Quintero
Cover copyright © 2017 by Hachette Book Group, Inc.

Hachette Book Group supports the right to free expression and the value of copyright. The purpose of copyright is to encourage writers and artists to produce the creative works that enrich our culture.

The scanning, uploading, and distribution of this book without permission is a theft of the author's intellectual property. If you would like permission to use material from the book (other than for review purposes), please contact permissions@hbgusa.com. Thank you for your support of the author's rights.

Little, Brown and Company
Hachette Book Group
1290 Avenue of the Americas, New York, NY 10104
Visit us at lb-kids.com

First Edition: June 2017

Little, Brown and Company is a division of Hachette Book Group, Inc.
The Little, Brown name and logo are trademarks of Hachette Book Group, Inc.

The publisher is not responsible for websites (or their content) that are not owned by the publisher.

ISBNs: 978-0-316-54640-9 (hardcover), 978-0-316-54636-2 (pbk.),
978-0-316-54641-6 (ebook)

Printed in the United States of America

LSC-C

Hardcover: 10 9 8 7 6 5 4 3 2 1
Paperback: 10 9 8 7 6 5 4 3 2 1

Contents

CHAPTER ONE
Hot Homework

BEEP! BEEP! BEEP! BEEP!

My morning alarm was blaring at full volume while I rolled around in bed, hoping it would go away forever. I needed to get up, get ready, and head to school, but I was too exhausted to move. When I finally reached to turn off the piercing sound, I noticed my little sister, Felicia, standing in the doorway of my room. She stared at me.

"GAH!" I shouted. "Get out of here! I'm in my underwear!"

"You're going to be late for school, Mr. Groggy Pants," Felicia said. She noticed the books and note cards spread out across my floor. "What is all of *this*?"

"I stayed up all night writing my lizard report," I explained, rubbing my eyes and yawning. I pulled a note card off the side of my face. Doing research for science class was hard work. "It's a major

part of my grade and has to be perfect. The teacher insisted we *hand*write it. Why couldn't we type it up like everyone else in this century? So lame."

"Ha! Yeah, *right*! You were probably playing video games all night," Felicia said.

"What? I wish! I was working on this report. See it right here?"

"Whatever." Felicia slammed the door shut and ran downstairs.

Sisters are so weird. I quickly threw on some clothes and marched down to breakfast, reading my report on the way to check for errors.

"Ooooh. Secret papers, huh?" my big brother, Gavin, said. He stared at my report like a hawk. He was up to no good, as usual. Dad was standing behind Gavin, using his flame powers to sizzle up a big pile of bacon. *Extra* crispy, just how I like it.

Everyone in my family has superpowers, by the way. It's pretty awesome—most of the time.

Felicia is super strong. (Last week, she lifted a dump truck over her head.) Gavin can create duplicates of himself. (His clones all think they know what they're doing, but they're all as dumb as the original.) Our littlest brother, Ben, can turn invisible (which makes *watching* him really hard).

But it's Mom and Dad who are the real heroes of the house. Dad is known as *Fireman!* He can create and control flames in an instant. They call Mom *Flygirl!* She can zoom across the sky in a flash. I hope to be like them one day.

Oh, I almost forgot to mention Grandpa Dale. He can fly and has super eyesight, and even has a long tongue that can snatch insects, which he sometimes eats. (So gross.)

As I went to sit down, Gavin snatched my science report right out of my hands. He waved it around like a maniac. "Give it back!" I shouted.

"These papers don't have secrets on

them. It's just some dumb schoolwork!"
Gavin said, whipping my report back and
forth in my face.

"Stop horsing around!" I shouted. But
it was too late. Gavin bumped into Dad's
flaming hand, and my handwritten report
caught fire in an instant. "Nooooooo!" I
moaned. "It took me all night to write that
paper."

Gavin was cackling like a hyena. "It's not funny, you jerk!" I shouted, punching him in the arm.

"Hey, no roughhousing, Peter. And, Gavin, it's not funny," Dad scolded. "You just lost all TV privileges for a month. Keep it up and we'll start locking you in a cage."

I usually loved Dad's sense of humor, but this time I hoped he was serious.

"He deserves to be in a cage!" I snapped. "It took me forever to write that report! What am I going to tell my teacher?! *THIS IS A NIGHTMARE!*"

"Keep your voices down," Mom said, joining us in the kitchen. "Ben and

Grandpa are still sleeping. Let's not wake them up, please."

I wished Grandpa was awake so he could tell me what to do. He's full of good advice. He's also full of *weird* advice. I never know what I'm going to get.

Wait a second. Did I forget to introduce the most important character in this story? I did. It's me! My name is Peter Powers. I have the ability to make ice cubes and freeze stuff. I used to think my power was pretty lame, but I'm finally getting the hang of it. I think I might even be getting stronger. I'm trying to learn how to develop my superpowers so that one day, I can fight injustice like my parents do.

For now, I'd have to settle for small stuff. Gavin needed payback. When he wasn't looking, I reached over and put my hand in his backpack. Using my super-powers, I filled it with ice cubes. Hah!

But when I looked back at the extra-crispy report, I felt sick to my stomach. Ice powers were cool, but I wished I had the power to travel back in time and stop Gavin from becoming a menace. "What am I going to do?" I muttered. "I have class in less than an hour. I don't have time to rewrite my paper."

"Tell your teacher the truth and explain the situation," Mom said. "You've still got your notes and research. Rewrite your paper tonight and turn it in tomorrow. Don't stress, okay, Peter? Everything will be fine."

"The truth? Miss Dullworth won't believe me," I said. "Maybe I could make up a story...."

"You better not *lie* to your teacher, Peter," Felicia sneered. "Or *bad* things will happen."

"Bad things are *already* happening," I grumped.

RUUUUUUMMMMMMMBBBBBBLLLEEE!

Suddenly, the ground began to shake, and our house swayed back and forth. Pictures fell from the walls, and one of Mom's old vases fell to the floor and shattered to pieces.

"An earthquake!" Mom said. "Everyone get in the doorway."

Once the tremor was over, Mom and Dad checked on Grandpa and Ben. Everyone was fine, so they jumped into action. "I'll hit the skies to survey the damage and make sure the people of Boulder City are safe," Mom said.

"You go high and I'll go low," Dad said,

grabbing his superhero costume from the laundry hamper.

"Looks like you kids are biking to school today," Mom added. "Have a good day!" Then she flew out the back door.

"Everyone grab some bacon and toast before school. Except Gavin. No delicious bacon for Gavin." Dad was definitely not joking that time. He *never* joked about bacon.

On my bike ride to school, I couldn't stop thinking about my science report. I'd worked so hard on it. *Maybe Dad is right*, I thought. *I'll just tell the truth*. What's the worst thing that could happen?

CHAPTER TWO
The First Fib

The bell rang as I rushed into the classroom, sweaty and out of breath. Miss Dullworth was too busy writing on the chalkboard to notice my tardiness. I sat down at my desk and waved to my two best friends, Sandro and Chloe.

"Today, we are talking about earthquakes," the teacher began. "As you all know, Boulder City had one this morning— though we *shouldn't* have. Boulder City isn't anywhere near a fault line. That means something strange is going on. But in this town, I guess that's normal."

As Miss Dullworth droned on, I was dreading the part where she asked everyone to turn in their science reports. Was I lucky enough for her to forget? (Nope.)

Chloe knew something was wrong with me. It's tough to hide my emotions from a super smarty-pants like her. "You still shaken up, Peter?" she asked.

"I know *I* am," Sandro said. "Earthquakes are freaky. Where were you when the shaking began?" He snuck a pretzel out of his pocket and into his mouth. He loves snacking.

"I was in the middle of a breakfast

meltdown," I whispered. "My science report got burnt to a crisp because my brother is about as smart as a shoe. I don't know what I'm going to do."

"Total bummer, dude!" whispered Sandro. "But enough about you. Aren't you going to ask me where *I* was during the earthquake?"

"Where were you?"

"I was on the toilet! *Duh*. I thought *I* was the one causing the earthquake. You should have heard the rumbles. My belly did *not* agree with last night's Tex-Mex," Sandro said. Chloe and I groaned. "What? You asked!"

"There's damage all over town, and

a big sinkhole opened up in the Chow Palace parking lot," Chloe whispered. "After school, let's take a look."

"Heck yeah!" said Sandro. "Have you tried Chow Palace's Lord of the Fries? They're the best chili cheese fries in town. It's like a tasty explosion in my mouth."

"Enough chitchat, class. Bring your science reports to my desk!" shouted Miss Dullworth. She seemed to be having a rough day so far. Her hair was a mess and her shirt was on backward. Her attitude, however, was as positive as it always was.

Sandro sauntered up to Miss Dullworth. "My dog ate my homework," he said.

Chloe and I rolled our eyes at such a lame excuse. "I know how that sounds, but it's true! I was eating beef jerky the whole time I wrote the report, and I guess it smelled like doggy treats, 'cause he chowed down on it."

"Likely story, Mr. Santiago," Miss Dullworth said. "You get a zero."

"But I'm telling the truth!" Sandro said. As he turned toward me and Chloe, he shrugged. "My mom's going to kill me. But don't worry. One day Sandro the Hungry shall rise again." Then he started doing all these weird karate-esque fighting moves. He spends *too much* time on the Internet.

Sandro told the truth and got a zero. What was I going to do? I couldn't fail!

"Peter, are you okay?" Miss Dullworth asked as I stepped forward. "You're sweating *a lot*." I'm a nervous sweater. When I get nervous, I have to try *not* to start popping out ice cubes. I have a secret identity to maintain! Still, *way* embarrassing.

"Where's your paper, Mr. Powers?"

"It's...it's..." I sputtered uncontrollably. "It's...my grandpa Dale. He's in the hospital. I didn't get to finish my paper because my whole family was with him last night...."

Oh no! Why did I just lie? I thought.

"I'm sorry to hear that, Peter. Would it help if you had some extra time to turn in your report?" Miss Dullworth asked. I nodded yes without a second thought.

"Take the time you need to get the work done," Miss Dullworth said.

I suddenly felt so relieved. I had lied and nothing bad had happened. This was awesome!

Then Miss Dullworth added, "Just make sure you get a signed note *from your parents.*"

Uh-oh, I thought. *Now I've done it.* As

I rushed back to my desk, my stomach began to growl. I think it was angry with me for lying.

"What did she say?" Chloe asked. "And why are you so sweaty? Did your ice powers turn wonky all of a sudden?"

"I just lied. *Big time*. I don't even know why I did it," I said. "I couldn't stop myself!"

"Not a good choice, Peter," Chloe said.

"I know," I said, dropping my head on the desk. What was I going to do?

Then, out of the corner of my eye, I saw it...a *LIZARD PERSON* staring at me through the window. He darted across the schoolyard and disappeared

into the woods before anyone else saw
him.

Great, I thought to myself. *I told* one
little lie, and now I've gone crazy.

CHAPTER THREE
The Hole in the Earth

Walking home from school with Chloe and Sandro, all I could think about was how I had lied to Miss Dullworth about what had really happened. I wondered how I was going to get out of this one. Was it too late to tell the truth?

"Did you know that geckos and chameleons love to eat crickets?" I said. "That fact was burnt to a crisp, just like all the other amazing facts in my report."

"Eating crickets? That's disgusting!"

Sandro winced. "But I'm so hungry right now, I'd probably eat some. I'd put bacon on 'em. And cheese sauce, of course. Maybe throw a hamburger in there for good measure. *Mmmm*, cricket burger..."

"Well, this earthquake hole will take your mind off your impending doom," Chloe said, trying to get me to smile.

We arrived at the former parking lot of Chow Palace. Now there was just a big hole. It looked like the earth had grown a mouth, and its teeth were made of rocks. Chloe knelt down and studied the opening. "Miss Dullworth was right— this is odd. This doesn't look like it was caused by an earthquake. It looks forced, as if something *dug* its way up here."

"What could be big enough to tear a hole in the earth and cause the entire town to feel it?" I asked.

"I have no idea," Chloe said. "But the three of us are going to find out."

I craned my head over the edge of the hole—and noticed a pair of blinking eyes staring back at me from the darkness.

"Uh…you guys…" I stuttered, stumbling backward. "We've got problems!"

"Howdy!" said the lizard man, who'd popped his head up from below.

The three of us screamed and started running. We had no interest in getting eaten like crickets. Sandro ran past Chloe and me, moving faster than I'd ever seen him. The three of us ran straight to my

house. I almost tripped over Gavin as we barged into the living room.

"Lizard...people...LIZARD...PEOPLE..." I huffed and puffed, grabbing Mom's arm like a maniac. "I saw one...at school...and another...just now...crawled out of the sinkhole....It thought...we were food!"

"Whoa, son," Mom said, always collected. "Take a deep breath, and then talk."

I explained everything. Then I added, "Lizards are cold blooded, so they don't like chilly temperatures. Which means I should have used my ice powers to stop them! But I didn't. I'm a terrible hero-in-training. The lizards are attacking and *I'm a failure!*"

"Peter, relax for a minute," Dad said.
"Are you sure you saw a lizard person?
We've had our fair share of strangeness
in Boulder City, but *that* sounds a little
far-fetched."

"He's telling the truth, Mr. and Mrs.
Powers," Chloe said.

"We should check it out, dear," Dad
said to Mom.

"Want me to help?"
Sandro asked. He made
a karate chop at the air.
"I've been practicing."

"I think we adults
have it covered," Mom
said. "You kids stay

inside, where it's safe. Mr. Powers and I will—"

"They're here!" Gavin said, pointing out the window. A handful of lizard people stood in our front yard, waving happily. They were tall and thin and covered in green scales. They didn't *look* like they wanted trouble—but they *were* lizard people!

"Kids, stay here," Dad said. "We're going to chat with our visitors."

"At least they aren't naked," Gavin noted.

"Are you out of your mind?" I said, grabbing Dad's arm. "They're lizards, Dad! They'll swallow you in a single gulp! I should know, I wrote a report on them."

"Peter, that's enough," Mom said. "Just because they're different from us doesn't mean they have ill intentions. Even lizard people deserve a chance to explain themselves."

Mom and Dad went outside to speak to the lizard people while the rest of us watched patiently from inside. After a few minutes, there was laughter and handshakes. What was going on? I expected a big battle!

"What happened?" I asked as soon as my parents walked in. "Are they going to take over the planet?"

"There's nothing to worry about, Peter," Mom assured me. "You'll see soon enough." She winked at Dad. They both giggled.

Was it possible that my parents had been hypnotized by the lizard people?

CHAPTER FOUR
City Visitors

The following day, the people of Boulder City gathered at city hall to hear a special announcement from the mayor. Something big was about to happen, and everyone could feel it. Everyone except for my siblings. They couldn't care less. Felicia whined about missing her new favorite cartoon, *Empress Warriorpants*, while Gavin was busy playing Snatch-E-Kins on his smartphone. Me? I was still worried about lizard people trying to eat us.

31

"Turn off your phone," Dad said as the mayor appeared on the steps of city hall.

"But I'm so close to snatching them all!" Gavin yelped. Dad took Gavin's phone and put it in his pocket.

"Welcome, citizens! Thank you for coming," the mayor began as the crowd fell silent. "Yesterday, a geological event shook our fair city to the core, and a delegation of Lizardians revealed themselves to the world. Some of you were alarmed, while others were concerned. It's time to put your fears to rest.

"The Lizardians come in peace! Before I introduce them, I want to extend a hearty thank you to Fireman and Flygirl. They were instrumental in assisting with the earthquake cleanup effort. We appreciate their service, wherever they might be!"

The crowd cheered loudly, not knowing that their favorite heroes—my parents—were standing among them in their secret identities.

"I hate that code name," Mom mumbled. "I'm not a *girl* anymore. I'm a full-grown woman."

"Why don't you change it?" I asked.

"I should. I didn't pick it. That's just what the news reporters started calling me, and it stuck like glue."

"Fireman's not much better," Dad

added. "That's what I get for letting a website choose my superhero name. A word of advice, Peter. Whatever you do, make sure *you're* the one who selects your code name. Otherwise you might get stuck with one you're not in love with."

"Noted!" I said cheerfully. My parents always have good advice.

"I'm proud to present our newest friends," the mayor said, "Lizardian Leader Lenn and the League of Lizards!" He welcomed a group of lizard people onto the stage. They seemed kind of goofy looking and were dressed like farmers with straw hats and overalls. *Maybe I was wrong to judge them so quickly,* I thought.

34

"Golly, Mr. Mayor. We sure are thankful that y'all have been so kind to us lizard folk. We're just so darn happy to be aboveground again. It gets pretty lonely *down south*," Lenn said with a thick twang. The crowd chuckled.

"We're happy to have you, Lenn," beamed the mayor.

"We've lived underground for a *long* time," Lenn said. "Shucks, it sure is drafty down there. But us cold-blooded creatures need a little warm sun every once in a while. Eatin' worms sure does get old. My stomach has been growlin' for some flies, mosquitoes, and a couple of delicious crickets. Would y'all mind if we stayed up top for a while and ate up all yer bugs?"

"I hate mosquitoes!" said a person in the crowd. "Me too," added another. "Eat all our flies," someone said. "Be our guest!"

Thunderous applause filled the air as the people of Boulder City went wild.

Lenn and his League of Lizards each gave a thumbs-up, flicking their forked tongues as the crowd cheered louder.

"We don't know that much about the Lizard League," Dad whispered to Gavin, Felicia, and me. "But we'll work together with them and build a partnership. It's important to welcome new people into your community. That's how everyone grows."

It sounded like a good plan, but the lizard people still creeped me out. I felt bad. Was I being intolerant, judging a book by its cover?

Grandpa wheeled over Dad's foot with his wheelchair. "I don't care what you say. I'm not gonna trust those whippersnappers."

"Dad! Don't be rude," Mom said to Grandpa.

"I'm not! I'm just old-fashioned. I don't trust *anyone* with a forked tongue. In my experience, anyone with a forked tongue is a *liar*."

A terrible thought occurred to me. I reached up to touch my tongue, to see if it had developed a fork now that I had lied. Thankfully, it hadn't. Not *yet*, anyway.

CHAPTER FIVE
Stop Talking

At school the next day, everyone was buzzing about the League of Lizards. People were curious and excited about their strange arrival. Some kids were spreading a rumor that the lizards were really humans in disguise and it was all part of some big publicity stunt. That seemed a little far-fetched to me. Sure, they had appeared out of nowhere, but the lizards seemed like they genuinely wanted to help. After the itchy insect invasion, we certainly could use some pest control around town.

After the bell rang, I was walking out of class with Chloe and Sandro when Miss Dullworth called out to me. "Peter? Can I see you for a moment?"

Oh no. With all the League of Lizards excitement, I'd completely forgotten about my report and the note from my parents and the whole lie situation.

"Hi, Miss Dullworth," I said. "I'm sorry to tell you this but...I don't have the note." It felt good to get that off my chest. But with her giving me the evil eye, I got nervous. And when I get nervous, I sweat and I talk. I should have stopped talking when I had the chance. "You see, my parents were so worried about Grandpa that they couldn't stop crying."

"Oh dear!" Miss Dullworth said.

I hadn't planned on telling another lie, but it's like I heard a sports guy in my head saying, *Go big or go home!*

"Yeah, there were so many tears. Grandpa isn't doing well. My parents were at the hospital all night. I stayed home so I could take care of my dear, sweet siblings, of course." I looked over at Chloe and Sandro. They were waiting in the classroom doorway. Chloe was shaking her head and mouthing, *Stop talking.*

"That is terrible," Miss Dullworth said,

putting her hand on her heart. "I can't imagine what you're going through, Peter. Stay strong, and if you need anything, just ask. But I will take your science report now, if you don't mind."

Not only did I not have the note, I had forgotten to rewrite my assignment. I couldn't believe this was happening. One lie led to another. I couldn't stop myself.

"You're never

going to believe this, but I left it at the veterinarian's office," I said.

"The vet?" Miss Dullworth said. "I thought you were at home?"

I'm caught! I thought. And for a second, I was relieved. But then more lies flew out of my mouth.

"Oh, well, that is, our family dog, *Gavin*, has really bad fleas. And ticks! Plus, he smells awful, so we took him to the vet, and he's sick too," I added. At least there was one true thing in there. Gavin did stink.

"*Uh-huh*," Miss Dullworth said. Doubt was creeping into her gaze. "Well, I need you to turn it in tomorrow. So please make

sure you bring it. *With* the note from your
parents."

I nodded politely and walked out of
class.

Chloe leaned over and whispered in
my ear. "This is going to end *very* badly
for you, Peter," she warned. "Think about
what you're doing."

"You should have given her some
money," Sandro said, chuckling. "My dad
says you can get away with *anything* if
you give people money."

"That's terrible advice, Sandro! And
it's *wrong*. All of this is wrong," Chloe
protested. "Peter, you need to come
clean and tell Miss Dullworth the truth.

Otherwise it's going to turn into an even bigger mess than it is already."

"Chloe, you're right," I said. "I'm going to tell the truth. But I think I'll do it tomorrow."

"Why tomorrow?"

"Because maybe by then some miracle will happen, and I'll find a way out of this mess."

CHAPTER SIX
Houseguests

I wanted only one thing in life—to be a superhero. I thought about it every single day. But being a hero is about more than just having superpowers. It's about standing up for justice and *truth*. I seemed to be having trouble remembering that part. How could I possibly be a hero after lying to my teacher so many times? What was I going to do?

The whole situation bummed me out. I came home that afternoon, ready to focus on rewriting my report, but Mom threw a wrench into my plans the minute I walked into the house.

"Peter, you remember Lenn, don't you?" Mom said, sitting at the kitchen table with the leader of the Lizard League and his family.

"Uh...I...um...yes?" I stuttered. Lizard people were in my house. *Calm down, Peter*, I thought. *They're probably very nice.*

"This is his wife, Lana, and their twin boys, Lonnie and Bob. The mayor asked a handful of local families to host our new friends until they can find places to live. Lenn, Lana, Lonnie, and Bob will be staying with us for a few weeks."

At first, I thought my parents must be crazy for taking in Lenn and his family, but then I thought about what Dad said. We had to make our guests feel welcome and accepted. Once we got to know one another, we might even find out we're not so different. *That's* what being a hero is all about. I decided it was time to embrace the lizard people.

"HELLO, DEAR FRIENDS!" I exclaimed, hugging Lenn, then Lana, then Lonnie, and finally Bob. Bob seemed annoyed. He also didn't look like a little boy. But what did I know about Lizardians? "Welcome to the Powers family! Make yourselves right at home. Does anyone need a refreshment? The bathroom is down the hall on the right, and there are bugs all over the backyard if you're hungry. *Mi casa es su casa!* That's Spanish for 'My house is your house.'"

Mom smiled. I could tell she was proud of me. "I'm glad you feel that way, Peter," she said.

"Of course!" I replied cheerfully. "Being nice is its own reward. And friends really are the best presents. I read that on a pillow once. I'm not sure I understand what it means, but I just love it, don't you?"

The lizard people shook their heads.

"Speaking of pillows, hope you don't mind lizard slobber on yours," Gavin said to me. "'Cause Lenn's family is staying in *your* room."

"Yeah, right." I laughed nervously. But when I saw Mom's face, I realized Gavin wasn't kidding. "Wait, *seriously*?"

Mom didn't miss a beat. She grabbed Gavin and me by the shoulders and squeezed, which meant, *Don't freak out.* "Yes, seriously. Lenn and Lana will stay in your room."

Gavin pointed at me and laughed.

Then Mom added, "And Lonnie and Bob will stay in Gavin's room. He'll bunk with Felicia."

Gavin's eyes widened with anger and his face turned red. "WHAT?! UGH! THIS IS NO FAIR!" he whined, stomping off in a huff.

"So, um, where am *I* sleeping?" I asked.

"You'll be sleeping in Grandpa's room. I already made him promise to light a scented candle so it doesn't smell like broccoli soup," Mom said.

"Gee, Mrs. Powers, y'all are so nice to us lizard folk," Lenn said, flicking his lizard tongue all around. "We couldn't ask for a nicer host family."

"We're happy to do it, aren't we, Peter?" Mom said. She squeezed my shoulder again.

"Yup. Soooo happy," I said, forcing myself to smile.

After I gathered some clothes and a sleeping bag, I went to Grandpa's room. Grandpa was my best friend in the whole world—but staying in the same room with him? *That* was another story. Some-times he farted without knowing it. And it smelled like something died. (Probably from eating bugs and who knows what else.) I knocked on Grandpa's door and poked my head inside.

"Come in quickly, Peter!" Grandpa said

in a loud whisper. "Close the door behind you real tight. It's hot out there. Your mom turned off the air-conditioning for those lizards."

"They seem nice," I said, sitting down at the end of Grandpa's bed and letting out a lengthy sigh.

"Exactly. They *seem* nice," Grandpa said. "Doesn't mean I trust 'em."

SNIFF. SNIFF.

The room smelled like a fart. Grandpa's were often *silent, but deadly*.

CHAPTER SEVEN
Brotherly Advice

After dinner, I followed Grandpa to his room. As I rolled out my sleeping bag on his floor, Grandpa revealed his secret stash of cookies. "Bedtime's always better with cookies," he said, smiling.

I couldn't hold my guilt in any longer. I burst out, "Grandpa, I have to tell you something."

"If it's about my toots, *I know*," he said. "I may not feel 'em coming, but I can certainly smell 'em. They're awful. Sorry."

"No, it's about something else," I said, getting up and pacing around the room. "I told a lie, and it's eating me up inside!"

Grandpa had been around awhile and was full of advice. I was hoping he might have some that could help me out. "*Hmmm.* Did someone ask you how your

day was and you replied, 'Just fine,' when you meant to say, 'Terrible'? If that's the case, don't sweat it! That's just a little *fib*. They happen sometimes."

"No, I told a *BIG* lie. *To my teacher.* I'm ashamed of myself over the whole thing," I said, exasperated. "I didn't have my science report, so I told my teacher a lie to cover my tail. I was even going to forge a note from Mom and Dad! And the worst part is, the lie was about you being in the hospital...."

Grandpa stood up quickly, his feathery wings exploding from his back. He flapped into the air and waved his wings at me. "Hospital?! I'm in the prime of my life!"

he said, swaying back and forth. "Ooof. That made me a little dizzy. I'm going to sit back down now."

Gavin swung the bedroom door open. Apparently, he'd been listening at the door. "You feel *guilty*, Peter?" he asked. "Telling a lie isn't *that* big a deal. I do it all the time. Nice *jammies*, by the way."

"Thanks!" I said. My pajamas were brand-new, so I took the compliment.

"That was a lie," Gavin sneered. "See? It's *easy* to lie."

"But it's not honest!" I said. "I'm ending all my lies tomorrow morning. I'm going to tell the truth. No more lying. *Never.* Not even if it's an emergency."

"Don't say *never*, Peter," Grandpa said. "Sometimes you have to lie. Like when your lady love asks if you like her dress. Even if you hate it, you have to say something nice."

"Stop freaking out, kid brother," Gavin said. "You just have to learn the *right* way

to tell a lie. One: Always look your opponent right in the eyes. Two: Smile big. And three: Never stutter. If you stutter, people will know you're nervous. Speaking of nervous, try not to sweat so much when you lie. That's a telltale sign. Remember those rules and you'll be golden."

"But I don't *want* to lie," I countered.

"Attaboy," Grandpa said. "You stay good, Peter. Even if it means failing a class."

Gulp. But if I failed, Mom and Dad would ground me for sure. Why was there no easy way out?!

"Trust me, it *works*," Gavin said. "You know what? I'll even write your note from the parents. I've been practicing Dad's handwriting for years." He quickly darted off in a flurry of excitement.

I started to get butterflies in my stomach.

Forging a note from Mom and Dad didn't
feel right, but what else could I do? I
didn't want to fail. I turned to Grandpa,
hoping he'd help me figure out a better
solution. But he was already fast asleep
and snoring like a bear.

Prrrrrrttttttt!!!

Grandpa's toot rang out like a trumpet.
I tucked myself in and tried not to breathe
through my nose.

CHAPTER EIGHT
Midnight Surprise

I'd been lying in bed for hours, but I couldn't sleep. Too much stuff was on my mind. I couldn't stop thinking about my big mess of lies. Did I really think that giving my teacher a forged note would solve my problem? I sure as heck didn't have any answers.

What I really needed was a good night's rest. Instead I was sleeping on the floor of my grandpa's room. He wasn't a sleep-walker, but he sure was a sleep*farter*.

And it was really hot in his room. It appeared that Mom had raised the temperature in the whole house to accommodate our Lizardian houseguests. What I needed was a tall glass of milk. That always made me sleepy.

I quietly went to the kitchen. As I approached, I heard strange noises. Two figures in the darkness were hissing at each other. It was Lonnie and Bob! They were carrying large bags from the backyard, through the kitchen, and into the basement. Part of me wanted to wake Dad up and tell him what was happening. But if it was a false alarm, I'd get in trouble. *What would a hero do?* I wondered. The League of Lizards were our new friends, so it wasn't as if they were up to something bad. Or *were* they? I had to make sure, so I flipped on the lights.

"Hey there!" I said as Lonnie and Bob stopped dead in their tracks. They were so surprised that they almost dropped their cargo. "What's going on here?"

Bob looked me up and down. "None of your business, kid," he scoffed. Lonnie and Bob went back to work, but I wasn't done with them just yet.

"It kind of *is* my business," I said, "since it's my house and all. So tell me what you're doing—please." I was surprised at how good I was becoming at laying down the tough talk. Mom would've been proud, especially since I said please.

"Wanna bet?" Bob said, punching his fists together. He definitely didn't look like a kid to me now. He looked like an angry, short lizard adult.

"Well, hey there, Peter!" Lenn said, appearing at the basement door. He stepped in front of Bob, giving him a dirty look. But then he smiled for me. "It sure is *late* for a li'l boy to be awake. What're you doin' up?"

"I needed a glass of milk. What are *you* two doing moving heavy bags through the house in the middle of the night?" I asked.

Lenn smiled a big smile and made sure to look me square in the eyes. "Well, we're just so gosh-darn thankful to your folks for putting us up that we decided to plan a fun surprise for tomorrow. It'd be a tootin' shame if it got spoiled. You won't tell yer pappy about this, will ya, Peter?"

Now I felt bad for giving them the third degree. Sure, Bob was a little rough around the edges, but Lenn was as nice as could be. Plus, I loved surprises! Who doesn't love surprises? But I had to keep my cool.

"Surprises! I love surprises!" I said. My mouth sure had a mind of its own. "I won't tell anyone, Lenn. Don't you worry. Your secret is safe with me."

"Aw, thanks, Peter," Lenn said. "Now, you run on back to bed and rest up! It's going to be a big day tomorrow. Remember—*SHHHHHH*! Don't tell."

At first I had been skeptical of Lenn and the League of Lizards. I thought they were up to no good just because they looked different. But the more I thought about it, the more I realized that I was being unfair. Lenn and his family were planning a cool surprise for my family. What a nice thing to do!

"Night, Lenn!" I said, heading back to bed.

I never did get that glass of milk, but I didn't care. Yet as I drifted off to sleep, trying to think of tomorrow's big surprise, I found my brain wandering back to what Gavin had said about how to lie well. But why was I thinking of that? *Who* cares? I thought, then drifted off to sleep.

CHAPTER NINE
The Note

I can do this, I told myself again and again. So why was I sweating like a crazy person? After all, I *had* to do it. There was no other choice. It was time to get things over with.

As I walked into Miss Dullworth's class, I handed her the forged note. Gavin's handwriting looked *exactly* like Dad's. There was no way she'd know the difference. Miss Dullworth read it immediately. Her hand reached up to her heart, and she said, "Oh dear. Peter, I didn't know you were *adopted*."

I swiped the note from her hands and read it myself—which I should have done *before* I handed it to her. (Why had I trusted Gavin?) As soon as I read it, I felt my face flush red.

The forged note said my grandpa was in the hospital (a lie). It said our family dog was at the vet (another lie). And it also said this:

"P.S. Miss *DULLS*worth. Please take it easy on Peter. He just found out he is adopted. Thanks!"

I wanted to scream. I am *not* adopted!! I look just like Dad *and* Mom! It was another lie, and now I would have to keep up that lie to protect the other lies! This was exhausting!

"*Gavin*," I grumbled. *The next time I see him, I'm going to freeze his face off*, I thought. Miss Dullworth was giving me a strange look, so I turned on my famous Peter Powers charm and used Gavin's lie technique. I stared directly into her eyes and smiled. Without a stutter, I said, "Yes, I *am* adopted, my grandpa *is* in the hospital, and my dog *is* at the vet."

"Peter, I know. It's written in the note you just gave me," Miss Dullworth said. "Can I have the note back now?"

"Of course!" I laughed, handing it to

her. "Silly me. I just wanted to make sure everything was spelled correctly. My father has had *so much* on his mind, you know."

"You seem to be handling everything very well. I'm proud of you," Miss Dullworth said. "Let me know if you need any more time completing your assignments. The other students can help put together a study guide if you think it would help. *Anything* you need, Peter. We're all here for you during this difficult time."

Miss Dullworth was never this nice. I felt awful. Why couldn't I stop lying? I wasn't behaving like a hero *at all*.

"Thank you," I said. "It has been a very

long week, but I'm finding out *a lot* about myself."

"That's what happens during troubling times," Miss Dullworth said. "You find out the kind of person you are and the kind of person you want to be."

I nodded quickly and went to my seat, where I proceeded to feel *terrible*. I hoped that this was my last lie ever.

Wait a minute, I thought. *I just lied the way Gavin told me to. Eye stare. Smile. No stutter. Just like Lizard Lenn last night.* What if *he* was lying about the fun surprise? What if he was actually planning some sort of *evil* surprise?

I had to warn Mom and Dad.

CHAPTER TEN
Home Invasion

I stomped up to the front door of my house. I was ready to freeze Gavin in place over the note he wrote. I was furious! But when

 I grabbed the door handle, it was stuck. I pushed with all my might. The door wouldn't budge.

Is this another one of Gavin's pranks? I wondered.

"What's the matter?" Gavin said. He was returning home from school at the same time as Felicia. "Open the door. I'm starving."

"You're up to something, aren't you?" I said, pointing at Gavin. "This is a *joke*, isn't it? I bet I'll open the door and something bad will happen!"

"I don't know what you're talking about," Gavin said. I really wanted to turn him into a giant ice cube, but using our powers in public, without wearing a costume, was a big no-no. I wasn't about to get in trouble over Gavin. He'd already ruined my life enough.

But then Gavin tried the door, and it didn't open. "What gives?" he asked.

"Out of the way, *weaklings*," Felicia said, pushing us aside. She pushed on the door as hard as she could, but it still wouldn't budge.

FLAP! SWAP! WALLA WAUCKA SCHUCKTUNK! FLISH! FLASH! "HI-YAH!!!!!"

Loud fighting sounds and crashes were coming from inside the house. "Uh-oh. That's not good," Felicia said. The three of us ran to the window and looked inside. Grandpa was wrestling with two Lizard Leaguers.

"You won't take me down, you scaly little sneakers!" Grandpa wailed. One lizard person grabbed him by the ankles,

and another
gripped his arms.
They swung him
back and forth,
faster and faster,
toward the window.

"DUCK!" I shouted, yanking my siblings by the backs of their shirts and pulling them down.

The Lizardians opened the window and tossed Grandpa out. But they didn't know about his little secret. One second before Grandpa hit the ground, his gigantic wings burst out of his back and he swooped safely into the sky.

"WAHOO!" Grandpa exclaimed, zooming through the air. He loved showing off his loop-de-loop skills, even in the face of danger. "You can't keep me down!"

"Grandpa is awesome," I said. Felicia nudged my arm. The Lizardians were using hammers and nails to lock the windows to our house. Nothing was getting in or out.

"Dad, get down from there!" Mom shouted to Grandpa. She and Dad had just arrived, after picking up Ben from day care. "Someone will see your wings!"

Grandpa landed, shaking his fist in the air. "My wings aren't the problem! I knew this day would come. The Lizardians are taking over!"

"What are you talking about, Dale?" Dad asked.

Before he could answer, we looked up and down the street. All of our neighbors had been pushed or locked out of their houses too.

A newly installed loudspeaker on top of our house sparked on. An announcement from Lizard Leader Lenn boomed from above. "The League of Lizards is taking over!" Lenn shouted. "The residents of Boulder City have been peacefully removed from their homes. We don't want no trouble, so y'all just move along. Find yourselves a new city. The League of Lizards declares that Boulder City belongs to us!"

Mom and Dad looked so angry, I thought they might explode. But there was little they could do with so many neighbors around—not without exposing their superpowers.

"This is *our* house," Gavin shouted. "You better not touch my video games!"

Lenn leaned out the second-floor window. "Y'all better get out of town, or else!"

"Or else *what*?" I shouted. "I know a couple superheroes who'll remove you in an instant. You might've heard of them? Flygirl and Fireman! I hear they live nearby. *Very* nearby. Some might say very *very* nearby."

Dad whispered, "Cool it, son. They're called *secret identities* for a reason."

Mom handed Ben to Grandpa and shouted, "Get out of my house before I remove you from it—*permanently*."

"You're more than welcome to try—*after* you've met our precious pet!" Lenn pulled out a strange horn and blew into it. Suddenly, the ground began to shake.

A hole opened up in the middle of the street. As the ground fell away, the biggest lizard I'd ever seen climbed out. It was as big as my school. It was a giant Gila monster!

"This is *Lumpy*. Ain't he somethin' else?" said Lenn. "Lumpy—DESTROY THE HUMANS!"

CHAPTER ELEVEN
Gila Monster Madness!

As the giant Gila monster crawled into the sunlight, he started glowing, as if the sun made him stronger.

"Uh-oh," I said. "According to my report, lizards get energy from the sun. And I think this super Gila monster is getting supercharged."

Lumpy the Gila monster let out a massive roar. Everyone in Boulder City heard it.

"That's so not good," Felicia said. "Mom, do something!"

"I'm on it," Mom said. She turned to Grandpa, saying, "Take Ben away, and fly him somewhere safe."

Mom and Dad ran into the garden shed so the neighbors couldn't see them. They pulled open their clothes to reveal their superhero outfits hidden beneath.

"The rest of you follow Grandpa on foot," Dad told Gavin, Felicia, and me. "And remember—stick together, and *safety first*."

I wasn't ready to retreat just yet. This was a chance to redeem myself after telling so many lies. It was time for Peter Powers to do his hero thing.

"Wait, I can help! I know stuff about lizards. Plus, ice cube powers! Please let me help," I pleaded.

"Now is *not* the time to discuss this, Peter," Mom said, taking off into the sky. She zoomed back and forth in front of Lumpy the Gila monster. He tried to catch her with his weird lizard hands. That only made him angrier. Lumpy swatted, batting her away like a ball.

Mom crash-landed in our neighbor's

yard, right in the flower beds he loved so much. "Well, that wasn't awesome," Mom said, trying to stand.

The giant Gila monster screeched again. It started to run toward the crowds of people in the street. They were about to get crushed when a huge wall of flame appeared. The giant lizard reared back.

Dad was on the scene!

Lumpy didn't like the fire. He scurried back in the other direction. But his tail smacked Dad, sending him flying into the city lake.

"Oh no! Mom and Dad need a minute to catch their breath," I shouted to my siblings. I pulled up my hoodie and put on my hero mask. "We need to distract the Gila monster so no one gets hurt!"

"I've got this!" Felicia said. She pulled on her hero mask and used her super strength to pick up a giant truck. Then she slammed it down on Lumpy's foot. The lizard howled in pain.

We weren't supposed to be using our powers, but I was happy to see Felicia rise to the occasion when she saw people in trouble. Next up—*Peter Powers to the rescue!*

But strangely, Gavin beat me to the punch. He pulled on his own hero mask and copied himself, making a dozen duplicates. Each one ran in a different direction to point people to safety, away

from the danger. "Since we're using our powers, I figure I should lend a *few* hands!" he said.

Both my siblings were acting like heroes all of a sudden, while I was nothing but a big liar. I hadn't even had a chance to show anyone what I could do! Then again, what *could* I do? I had ice powers, but they weren't that great. After all, ice cubes aren't much help against a giant lizard monster destroying the city....

CHAPTER TWELVE
A Frosty Foe

I rushed over to Mom to see if she was okay. She was still kind of zonked out from Lumpy's sucker punch. "He's big, and he's got a mean right hook," she said, rubbing her head. "I'm *definitely* going to be sore tomorrow."

Felicia pulled a giant oak tree from the ground and swung it like a bat. It hit the giant Gila monster right in the nose. Lumpy roared.

And then he raised his foot and slammed it down on my sister.

"Felicia!" Mom and I screamed.

But my sister was fine. She pressed upward with her super strength, lifting the giant lizard's claw.

"This beast messed up my favorite outfit," Felicia growled. "Now I'm really mad!"

"It seems our sister is not only super strong, but super *tough*," Gavin said. "Why do girls always get the coolest powers?"

"Focus!" I said. "We need to stop the Gila and the Lizardians."

"I have an idea, Peter—" Mom started.

I knew she'd ask me to use my superpowers, I thought.

Instead, Mom said, "You know *all about* reptiles, don't you? You wrote a whole report about them. How do we stop Lumpy?"

Okay, so maybe she didn't want me to use my ice powers—but using my brain was just as important. It could help save the day.

"Lizards are cold blooded," I said. "That means they thrive in warmth. You've got to get him somewhere chilly in order to throw him off. If you fly him into the upper atmosphere for just a minute or two, it might be enough to cool down his body temperature and calm him."

"That's *brilliant*, son," Mom said.

Faster than a speeding bullet,
Mom flew into the air. She grabbed
Lumpy's scaly neck and pulled him
into the sky.

A minute later, Mom and the Gila
monster returned, covered in a layer of
frost. Mom lowered Lumpy into the giant

hole he came from. He trudged away, back into the darkness.

"*Brrrrrr*." Mom shuddered. "You'd love it up there, Peter. It's just your temperature."

Dad floated down from the sky, covered in flames. "I'm knocked out for five minutes, and my family takes care of the giant lizard," Dad said with a smile. "Good job, everyone. Even if you kids were supposed to stay safe...."

"I was helping people!" Gavin said.

"And apparently I'm super tough," Felicia said. "You don't have to worry about me anymore."

"We'll always worry about you," Mom said. "But right now, we aren't done.

Lumpy has been dealt with, but the Powers family needs a plan to get the Lizard League out of everyone's homes."

Mom saved the city from the Gila monster, Dad's powers were supercool, Gavin had been actually helpful, and Felicia had leveled up...and what had I done? Practically nothing. This was totally lame.

And I was ready for action. I could feel my ice power tingling up and down my arms, through my hands, and into my fingertips. Slowly but surely, my entire body became energized with the power of ice.

"You heroes may have defeated Lumpy,

but y'all can't do *nothing* to us!" Lizard Lenn announced from inside our house. His voice was trembling, and he seemed a little bit scared. "We ain't budgin' and you can't make us!"

"That's it," Mom said. "I want them out of our home!" She was ready to kick down the door. But I grabbed her.

"Let *me*," I said with a grin.

CHAPTER THIRTEEN
Icebox

"Stand back, everyone," I warned. "It's time for *MISTER CHILLZ, THE FROST KING OF BOULDER CITY*, to show these lizards *what's up!*"

"That's the *worst* superhero name of all time," Felicia sniped. "And way too long."

"I was just trying it out," I said.

"Remember what I said about code names?" Mom said. "*Think it through.* You never know what'll stick. Either way, I love you, my clever little guy."

"Mommmm! Not when I'm trying to be a hero!" I said.

My whole body was pulsing with ice power. It was more than I'd ever felt before in my whole life. It was really cool! But there was no time to waste. I placed my hands on the door to our house and concentrated.

Tiny icicles began forming around my hands. They spread across the outside of the house until the whole thing was covered in a layer of fresh frost. I was making the entire house as cold as a freezer.

A commotion erupted inside our home. Lizard Lenn and his friends were shouting like crazy. I didn't let it distract me. My job was to focus on the task at hand and keep my ice power going.

SMASH! CRASH! KERPLUNK!

Lenn and his Lizardian family tore through the boarded-up front door. They fell all over one another trying to escape the freezing-cold house.

"S-s-s-s-o c-c-cold in-n-n-n there," they said with chattering teeth and body shivers. "We g-g-g-give up!"

"Great plan!" Dad said. "Lizards *hate* the cold. Peter turned the house into one big fridge and drove them out. *Brilliant* idea, son."

Getting a compliment from Dad was

one of the best feelings in the world. But as soon as he slapped me on the back, I fainted. Yup, I was out *cold*.

I guess using my powers like that really took its toll on me. When I finally woke up, my parents (as their superhero alter egos) and the police had rounded up the rest of the Lizard League and were escorting them to police vans.

"We believed in you, Lenn. We trusted you," Fireman said. "Why'd you do it?"

"I'm so ashamed about this here mess. We didn't mean to do y'all any harm, sir," Lenn said. "We just got so sick of living in those cold, dark caverns underground. And y'all have such nice warm houses up here. I guess we thought the League of Lizards could take 'em and y'all could find new places to live. Sounds silly now that I say it out loud."

Flygirl shook her head. "But why lie once the people of Boulder City welcomed you into their homes?" she asked. "Why didn't you just tell them the truth from the beginning?"

"I wish I knew," Lenn said, shaking his head. "Lyin' is what us Lizardians are good at, I reckon. Never trust anyone with a forked tongue, I always say."

"TOLD YA!" Grandpa shouted.

CHAPTER FOURTEEN
Honest Lunch

At lunch the next day, I was on top of the world. I had helped save my hometown from a Lizardian takeover! Lots of people were checking out my big smile and jaunty strut. I was pretty noticeable. I found my friends and plunked my tray down, accidentally splashing gravy on my shirt. Of course.

"Well, well, well! Someone has got some serious swagger in his step today," Sandro said.

"So are you going to tell us what happened?" asked Chloe. "Or are you just going to grin all day long? You look so happy, I'm starting to get concerned."

"I love smiling," I said. Then I leaned in close to whisper to Chloe and Sandro. I needed to keep my voice down since my family had a secret identity to protect. "Yesterday was so amazing. I used my ice powers to drive the Lizard League out of my house. It turns out they lied about some stuff. Of course, if they told the truth, it might've saved them from the wrath of CHILLICUS REX!"

I moved my eyebrows up and down for maximum effect.

"Wait. Is *that* supposed to be your code name?" asked Sandro.

"You need to seriously rethink that," Chloe added. "So where did Lenn and the League of Lizards end up anyway?"

"My parents and the police escorted them to their brand-new home in the desert," I explained. "It's the perfect spot for the Lizardians to lounge in the sun all day

long and eat as many bugs as they want. Bob and I are going to keep in touch."

"EATING BUGS?! THAT'S DISGUSTING!" Sandro snapped. But then he noticed a chocolate chip cookie on the floor. He scooped it up and stuffed it into his mouth. *"Mmm-crunch-mmm-gobble-mmm-free-cookie!"*

The bell rang.

"Time for class," Chloe said, tossing her trash and grabbing her book bag. "Peter, did you rewrite your paper?"

"I FORGOT TO REWRITE MY REPORT!!!" I shouted, slapping my forehead like a dummy. "I'm dead. I'm so dead. I'm really, really, *really* dead."

"Aw man, that's bad news!" Sandro said, leaning in close. "Are you going to lie about it again?"

Before I could answer, Chloe said, "Please tell me you learned a lesson from the League of Lizards. The truth will set you free, Peter."

I just smiled. It wasn't going to be easy, but I knew what I had to do.

CHAPTER FIFTEEN
The Truth Revealed!

The bell rang. I was sitting silently in my seat with my head down. Why were my hands sweating? Why was I nervous?

Maybe Miss Dullworth won't ask for my science report, I thought. *Maybe she forgot!*

It was a silly thing to think. Teachers remember *everything*. I don't know how they do it, but it's true. Maybe they're superpeople with mental powers and everything? Clearly I needed to calm down.

"Peter?" Miss Dullworth said, nodding

in my direction. I sheepishly looked up and pointed at myself. "Yes, you *are* the only Peter in this classroom. And the only person who has yet to turn in a science report."

I took a deep breath and stood up. Then I began my walk of shame. *Of course* there was even more sweat. Soon I was

face-to-face with Miss Dullworth. What else to do but dive in headfirst? I wanted to lie, but I knew better....

"Miss Dullworth, I would like to tell

you the truth," I said. "I did write my paper, and it was so good. But then my brother—who can multiply—took my paper, and my dad—who makes breakfast with his fire powers—accidentally burned my report with his flaming fingers. And then I was going to totally rewrite it, but my family—who are all superheroes—got all mixed up in that whole lizard-invasion thing. It was totally crazy. Did you see that big Gila monster on TV? His name was Lumpy, and my mom and sister totally beat him up. Unbelievable, right? But I was able to save the day with my knowledge of cold-blooded animals. *That's* what my science report was all about, by the way. After my family saved the city, we all went out for pizza. I ate so much that I fell asleep as soon as I got home. What I'm saying is that I completely forgot about rewriting my report. Oh, and my brother forged that note. And my grandpa is super wacky but totally *not* dying. I should have just told you the truth in the first place, but I didn't and I'm sorry."

Miss Dullworth stared at me. I couldn't tell if she was angry or confused. I decided to break the silence with a compliment. "Are those new earrings you're wearing?" I inquired. "They're very, *um*, earring-y!"

"Seriously, Peter?" Miss Dullworth said with a dramatic eye roll. "Do you honestly

expect me to believe all of that nonsense?
A smart student like you should know
better. I don't appreciate being lied to. I'm
giving you a week's detention."

"I figured," I said.

Miss Dullworth handed me a detention
slip. "I suggest you visit the guidance

counselor. Based on what you've just told me, I'm concerned that you may not be living in reality, Peter. Get some *help*, okay?"

"Thank you, Miss Dullworth!" I said. "And believe me when I tell you that I'm still going to get you that science report. No matter the cost!" I *loved* using heroic language.

Once I was back in my seat, a gigantic grin mysteriously appeared on my face. Even though my teacher didn't believe me, it felt really good to get the truth off my chest. Lying made me feel so nervous and fearful. I finally felt free, like a weight had been lifted from my shoulders. Not only that, but my abilities were changing. I'd graduated from being able to wiggle a single ice cube out of my pinkie, that's for sure. And the good news is that I was just getting started. My powers were getting stronger, *and* I learned a valuable lesson about telling the truth. This adventure was a big win for FREEZY FROSTBITE, THE BOY WITH THE ICY TOUCH!

Hmmm, I thought. *I still need to work on that superhero name.*

"Peter, detention?! You are so grounded!" Chloe said.

"I doubt it," I said. "My parents can't get mad at me for telling the truth. In fact,

I have a question for them: If good guys aren't supposed to lie, then why do we lie about our secret identities?"

I couldn't wait to see if my parents had an answer for that one.

Meet PETER POWERS!

A boy whose superpowers are a little different from the rest...

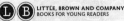

and the
Sinister Snowman
Showdown!

What would YOU do if you won the lottery?

Join the kids of Classroom 13 for their first misadventure in a new series!

lb-kids.com